VENGEANCE OF JUSTICE

Muhammad Ayyaan

ISBN
Paperback 979-8-89446-628-6
Hardcase 979-8-89475-637-0

The place where I grew up was the village of Nandpur. It was divided into two parts. In the upper part of the village lived the Brahmins, and in the lower part lived the Dalits. My real name was Gopal. However, it was later changed to Gopi. I was named Gopi because Gopal was the name of the son of Nandpur's richest Landlord, Rameshwar Singh. My father was told to change my name to Rameshwar Singh. Because my father worked in his field as a Labourer. Two options were given to my father; one was to leave his job, and another was to change my name. My father took the second option, and he changed my name, and I was made Gopi from Gopal. There were seven members in our family: my father, Ramlal, my mother; Geeta, my grandfather; Harilal, my grandmother; Lata, my younger sister; Kamla, my younger brother; Deepu and me, Gopal, I mean Gopi. My father Ramlal was the one and only bread-earner of our family. My father worked 13 hours a day. He left the home at six and came back at seven. My father was able to afford only bread for two times for our family. I was the elder child of my family from my childhood days. I was told that when you work, then you would get the bread. When you do not work, you would die, and no one would even ask you. When I was a child, I didn't pay attention to these talks. I was just roaming the village here and there with my friends. We always wanted new clothes because our clothes were ragged and dirty because we were playing in the sand the whole day. Our feet were dirty, and there were a lot of wounds on them because we were always barefoot. We didn't have slippers even though we didn't know what slippers were. One morning, my father told me that today is a function at my saiths house, and he told me to come for help, so I am taking you with me. I was very happy because I thought I would eat a variety of things there. When we reached the saiths house, I took my head up. It was so big that it might touch the sky, I thought. My father advised me to be quiet and not to disturb anyone. When we entered, there was a big garden, and there was a sweet smell of flowers all around. In the meanwhile, the saith came. My father touched his feet, and he told me to touch his feet. When I took my hand towards his feet, he kicked me. My father didn't give any attention to me. He put his head on his feet and started asking for forgiveness. The saith replied this boy had dirty hands, and he was going to make my shoes dirty. Then he asked Ramlal to go inside and give water to the guests and take your son. He told him to be quiet and not to talk with any guests. My father came, and he took me with him. I was quiet and was surprised at what was happening. When we reached the front door, my father took me to the side and started crying. His tears made my shoulder wet. I was not saying anything. Might there be a padlock on my lips? My father told me, Son, are you fine? I got frantic and started disputing with my father. I asked when the saith kicked me; you were asking him for forgiveness and didn't even see me, and this time, you are asking are you fine? My father told me that he would be fired from the job if he didn't do so and started saying sorry to me. I got emotional when I heard these words from my father. My father told me if anything is done to us, we have to endure it. We can't do anything. We are Dalits. After hearing these words from my father, I got emotional. I was not able to understand the situation. My father took me with him to the gatekeeper's hut at the entrance of the house. There was the gatekeeper, Bansi Chacha, my father's friend. My father told Chacha that I was going inside and that I was leaving my son here, so please take care of him. Chacha agreed, and my father told me to sit there. I didn't ask anything and sat on the bench. Chacha was outside and was opening the gate for the guests. I was sitting on his bench inside the cabin. I was able to see everything clearly. The people were passing by. I was seeing the ladies wearing shiny sarees whose shine was falling on the window glasses. Then I was thinking about my mother's saree, the ragged, having a big hole at the back. There was a beautiful smell of perfumes all around. The kids were wearing new clothes, and then I was looking towards mine. After some time, when the rush decreased, Chacha came inside. He told me that when the guests eat lunch, we will go inside and have lunch. He also told me that whatever I like, I can eat; no one will stop me. Then he asked if I would come with me. I nodded my head. He again went outside. I started thinking, is Chacha kidding me, or is he telling the truth that we can eat anything we like, and no one will stop us from eating the dishes? I started wandering about the dishes that I was going to eat inside. I started making the list of the dishes in my mind, but I didn't exactly know the names of the dishes. I had just heard about the names of some dishes somewhere, but I had not even seen a single of them in my whole life. In the meantime, a lady entered from the gate with her two kids, a boy and a girl. When I saw her, they were totally white, and they were wearing clothes that I had not even seen before. I was surprised to see the white people. When they reached the lawn, the saith came bare-footed and started welcoming her. I was surprised by the angry saith welcoming a lady. I wanted to know who the lady was. Saith was also welcoming her kids by giving them sweets to eat. I thought if I became white, then the saith would also respect me and would give me sweets to eat. I didn't know how to become white. After some time, Chacha came. He told me that the guests had finished the lunch and we had to go inside to do the lunch. I asked him if Baba was there. He replied yes, he was inside. I was not interested in the lunch; I just wanted to become white. When we reached the gate, the people were coming out from the gate, so we stood aside. From the window, I saw some ladies in the room who were applying something from a bottle on their faces, and they were getting white. I thought this was the way of getting white. When we entered, I just wanted to enter that room and apply that thing on my face to get my face white. The people went out, and we entered the house. When I saw it, it was very big. There were big lamps made of glass hung all around, which made it beautiful. There were many rooms, and guests roamed here and there. I just wanted to locate that room. In the meantime, my father came. He took me with him inside the kitchen. When I saw everything was finished and nothing was left for us. I told my father where lunch was. He replied that so much food is stuck on the utensils, we will get it, and we will do the lunch with it. I got furious and ran away from the kitchen. I reached the lobby, and I located the make-up room. There were many ladies around it, so I sat on a bench near the room. After some time, the temple bell rang, and everyone started going for the pooja. I thought this was the perfect chance to enter the room. I first went to the door and started walking here and there. When I was assured that no one was seeing, I went in. It was a small room, but there were mirrors on all the walls. There were almirahs and tables. When I walked to the front mirror, I opened the almirah's door. I took some bottles and started applying them to my face. My face started getting white, but it was irritating me. Suddenly the door opened, and a lady entered, and when I saw her, I got nervous. She started shouting choor choor. The crowd gathered, and the saith came. He shouted at me you son of a pig! How dare you enter this room. He started beating me. In the meanwhile, my father came. He started requesting the saith to forgive me, but he did not. He was continuously beating me. Somehow, he left me, but he fired my father from his job. My father started requesting him not to do this thing, but he fired him from the job. The saith ordered his guards to kick us out. Bansi Chacha was seeing everything. Perhaps he was my father's best friend, but he could not do that because he was also like us. We were kicked out by the guards. When we reached the road, my father pulled my leg and started beating me. Meanwhile, my father's uncle Nirupam Chacha came. He saved me. My father told him what had happened. He replied Gopi is just a kid. He doesn't have a sense of good and bad. You shouldn't beat him. Karma will hit the saith back. My father replied, but I have lost my job. How will I manage? Nirupam Chacha replied don't be sad. You will definitely get a job anywhere else. Nirupam chacha went away. My father and I started walking home, but he was not talking to me. We reached home. My mother asked whether you had bought the food from your saiths house, there is nothing left in the kitchen. Everyone is hungry. My father replied that due to this ka bhakt, I lost my job. My mother was surprised when she asked how our family would be run. We didn't have money to buy food. Everyone in our family was sad. I was making myself responsible for all of this situation. Late at night, my grandma came to me and asked Gopi Beta not to be sad, Ramlal. Get a new job, and everything will be fine. I asked what is the difference between the upper castes and us. She replied when you play the gulli danda, it has its rules. likewise, our society also has some rules, and we have to follow them. We can't violate any rule. Then she asked me to sleep. I was not able to sleep because my consciousness was hurting me. I was only weeping. The next morning, there was nothing for breakfast, and everyone was hungry. My mother went to our neighbour Shanti's house and bought some chapatis. All of us ate them without me, but my mother saved one for me. My father asked Shanti to give us breakfast, but she would not give us any time I had to do any job. My father asked me to eat this chapati. Your hunger will not give me a job. I asked nothing in return. When my mother told me several times to eat the chapati, she requested that I eat it. She smiled at me and went out. My father didn't get any job on the first day, so he sold a copper plate and bought some food. We ate the food for three days, but my father was not getting a job. He started selling kulfi in the streets but earned a little, which could give us food for only one time. After some days, a new kulfi shop was launched by the saith in the village to take revenge on my father. People started buying kulfi from the Saith's shop, and my father became unemployed again. My mother went to the saiths house to request him to forgive us, but he kicked my mother out and broke her arm. My grandfather took a loan from Nirupam Chacha to get medicines for my mother. My mother got ill. she took the bed. She was not able to do anything, and Hakim Sahab advised her to rest. My mother was ill, so Kamla and my grandma started performing the household chores. My father started working in a mill near our countryside. My father was working there and was getting a salary which gave us two times food and medicines for my mother. He was also saving money to pay the debt. After some time, we cleared the debt, and my mother was getting cured. One day, the saith heard that my father was working in the mill. He told the mill owner to fire my father. My father was again fired from the job. We didn't know what we had done with the saith of which he was taking revenge on us. The medicine stopped, and day by day, my mother's condition was getting worse. Our economic condition was also getting worse. My father went to sell the mungfali at the station. He earned a little, but my mother again got medicines, and after one month, she was cured. When the saith heard about it he got very frantic he went to the station with his workers and broke my father's leg and made him handicapped. After this incident, the only bread-earner in our family stopped earning. There was nothing left. My mother was recently ill, and she was not able to earn any money. My grandfather was very old, and he was also unable to do any job. My grandmother was always ill, so she couldn't do any jobs. My siblings were very little, and they could not get a job. We needed medicines for our father if the medicines would stop so he could die. I didn't have any other option without becoming a bread-earner for my family. I went to the station in search of a job. I noticed there is a shortage of coolies on the station. From the very next day, I started the job of a coolie on the station. In the whole day, I earned between Rs 85 and 95 on a general day. On the weekend, due to the rush, I earned Rs 95 to 100 a day. Day by day, I was getting exported in my work. Everything was going fine. I was able to give food to my family, and I was able to provide medicines to my father. After some months, my younger brother Deepu also came to work with me. We earned together. Our financial condition was slowly getting good. My father was slowly getting cured. But one day, Deepu and I were at the station, and our neighbour Vinod's son Ravi came. He informed us that our grandfather had died. We ran towards home. But he was already dead. We were going to do their antim sanskar in the Shamshan ghat. In the meantime, the saith came with his goons. He stopped my grandfather's antim sanskar. When I asked him why he was doing all this, he slapped me on my face. He asked Ramlal's son Gopi, who had spoilt the make-up of my wife, which was very costly. Till they do not pay me the cost of the make-up, I will stop the antim sanskar of Harilal. At that time, I did not have money because I had spent my savings on wood for the antim Zanskar. Nirupam Chacha came to the forefront, and he paid the cost of the make-up to the saith. He went away but spitted his paan on my grandfather's body. At that time, I got very frantic, but I couldn't do anything. When the antim sanskar was finished, I was not able to control my anger at that very time. I was roaming here and there. I didn't know what I had to do. I just wanted to take revenge on the saith. We came back to home. Everyone was remembering the moments spent with our grandfather. We were not having the shock of our grandfather's death; we were having the shock of the insult which was done to our grandfather's body. I realised that if I had not entered that room that day today, our family would be a happy family. But I was only frantic on the saith. I made a motive in my life that, at any cost, I would take revenge on the saith. After some days, I and Deepu again went to the station after few days. When we reached the station, we noticed that some new coolies had come, and they were not allowing the old coolies to work on the station. If anybody is raising any objection, they are beating him. We went to the coolie hut, which was on the left side of the station where the coolies stayed. We saw all the coolies were sad because there was no work left for them at the station. I sat down. The senior coolie of the station, Lalu Chacha, told everyone that we had only two options one was to fight for our rights, and the second was to leave the station. The new coolies were very strong, and they had beaten many of us, so everyone was frightened, and most of the coolies agreed to leave the station. I got up and told my colleagues that at least we should give it a try. We should ask them once not to disturb us. Everyone agreed with me. All of us went out of the hut. I was walking in front, and others were walking from the back. When we reached the terminals, the new coolies gathered together. Lalu Chacha asked them if we could work together and why they were pressuring us to leave the station. We have spent our whole life on this station. A new coolie came up and slapped Lalu Chacha's face and warned him not to talk about anything else. I told him how dare you slapped him. He came to me, took my collar in his hand, and slapped me. I got very frantic. In the meanwhile, the other new coolies started disputing with my colleagues. I saw the new coolies were beating my colleagues. I also slapped on the coolies face. We started fighting, and everyone started seeing us. The passengers made a circle around us, and there was a circus. I broke his head, and his hands and body got red by the blood. When his colleagues saw his situation, they took him and ran away. Everyone started clapping. Lalu Chacha was happy because I took his revenge. All the coolies started thanking me. From the very next day, we started our work again. By broking up the head of a strong man, I got much confidence in my motive, which was to take revenge on the saith. After two days, I worked at the station, and some policemen came to the station. I didn't pay any attention to them because it was a common thing at the station. After 2 or 3 minutes after their entry, they came to me and asked me are you Gopi I was surprised and nodded my head. They tied my hands tightly with a rope. The whole station gathered. Lalu Chacha asked them why they were arresting him. They asked the public two days ago if this person had broken the head of a person and today he died. He is a murderer. Everyone was shocked. Everyone told them they had started the fight, but they didn't pay attention to anyone. Deepu started weeping. I told him not to cry, but he didn't stop. They took me and put me in the police van. We reached to the police station. I was put in the lock-up. I saw in the lock-up there were many goons. Some of them were murderers, some were robbers, and some were gangsters. When I saw them, I got frightened because I had never seen any criminals. When I sat down, all of them started teasing me. They pulled my collar and tore my shirt. I was not able to adjust to the criminals. The next day, a police official came to me and informed me that tomorrow I would be submitted in front of a judge. He also told me that if I want to hire a lawyer, I can. If I can't, then the government will offer me a lawyer. I didn't know anything about these things. The other criminals told me that tomorrow, your punishment will be decided, and you will be transferred to jail. I was sad, not for myself but for my family. There was no one who would care for them. Deepu was not big enough to handle the whole house alone. I didn't sleep the whole night. The next morning, two police officials came and took me to the courtroom. On the way, they told me that I would be presented in front of a session judge who would decide my punishment. I didn't know what a session judge was. I asked them what my punishment would be. They replied it was in the hands of the judge. The judge will decide your punishment. They told me the government had also given me a lawyer. When we reached the court, it was a big building. I saw the people almost present there were wearing black clothes. I saw seeing here and there only. When we entered the courtroom, it was a room surrounded by chairs. The policemen put me in a cabin where I could only stand.

My lawyer came to me. He was a man of 30 wearing a black dress and a white shirt. He told me that he would do his best to save me. I touched his feet, and he smiled at me and went away. The judge came; he was an old man of about 60, having clear big white moustaches, and was wearing a black suit. When he entered the courtroom, everyone got up till he didn't ask to sit. No one sat down. He went and sat on his chair. I saw my lawyer and the other lawyer start a debate. At one point, the judge asked them to stop, but they again started, and a person sitting behind the judge was only writing something on the typewriter. Finally, the judge asked the lawyers to stop the debate and asked them to sit down. Then, the judge took a small wooden hammer in his hand and struck it three times on a wooden piece on his table. Then he told everyone that the decision of the court was that Mr Gopi had committed a crime, which was clear, so he should be transferred to the district jail, and his punishment would be eight years, and his next hearing would be six months later. The judge told me all this in English, and I was not able to speak or understand English, so I didn't know what he was saying. After some time, two cops came to me, and they told me about my punishment. I begged them that I wanted to meet my lawyer because I had trust in him and that he would get bail for me. They called my lawyer. This time, his reaction was totally different from the first one. He told me that the court had given me a sentence of 8 years, but on my next hearing, he would do everything to get bail for me. I was shocked because I had many expectations of him. He asked me for the best of luck and went away. The cops tied me by hand and took me with them. They put me in a vehicle, and we went on the way to the district jail. They told me the jail was about 50 km away, so we would reach after an hour. They advised me to enjoy this one hour because I will see the world after six months on my next hearing. I didn't get their point, so

I asked them what they meant. They replied you would be put in jail, and you wouldn't be able to come out of jail. I was shocked to hear these words from policemen. I saw on the upper right side of their uniform their name was written with some stars. Everybody had a different number of stars. I asked one of the policemen what the stars on your uniform represented. He smiled and replied these stars determine the rank of a policeman. We reached to the jail. When we came down, I didn't see any buildings. I just saw very big walls that surrounded the land. I noticed there was only a door between the walls. The policemen again tied my hands, and we went towards the door. I saw there were policemen all around, and they saw me in a bad manner. There was a bad smell all around because the jail was near a dumping site. When we reached the door, the guards checked me, gave me a piece of paper, and asked me to put my signature on it. I didn't know how to sign, so they put my thumb in the ink and then put a stamp of it on the paper instead of the sign. The guards pushed the door, and when it opened, it made an irritating loud sound. We went in. The policemen took me to the jailer, who was a man of 50 with a strong body and a long black moustache wearing a police uniform. He asked me, you murderer, now you will be punished. The policemen who bought me gave some papers to the jailer and went away. The jailer rang the bell on his table, and suddenly, two cops entered. The jailer ordered them to take me for a medical examination. One among the two came ahead, took my hand tightly, and told me that now I would be medically examined to ensure that I was completely healthy or not. I was keenly listening to every talk, but everything was totally going beyond my understanding. The jailer looked up, with a silly grin, to me and told the cops to take me away. The cops took me in a van to the hospital. When we reached the hospital, the people present there started only seeing me, which made me totally uncomfortable. After the check-up, I was considered completely healthy. After the medical check-up was done, the cops took me back to the jail and entered the room of the jailer. The jailer ordered them to put me in bark no. 73, gave me the jail uniform, and allotted the prisoner code to me, which was 654. Both of them nodded their heads and took me with them. They took me with them, and we went to another room. The room was full of shelves, but there were only the same clothes on all the shelves. A man came to me, and he started measuring the size of my clothes. He started finding the uniform of my size on a shelf. He bought one for me and asked me to wear it. The uniform is full white, with blue stripes on the shoulders and on the cap. I wore it, and it was not good. It was very broad, and I was totally not comfortable wearing it. I asked them if I could wear my old clothes instead of this uniform. One of the cops gave an evil smile to me and said to me this is not your home. You are a murderer, and you have to wear this uniform until you are here. They gave me a plastic bag and told me to fold my old clothes and put them in the bag. I did the same. They took me out of the room to another room, which was full of lockers. One cop opened one locker and put the bag in it. They came up with a sticker and pasted it on the upper side of my shirt. I didn't know what was written on it. One cop told me that it was my jail code, and I had to remember it because it was my identity on the jail premises. I got completely depressed after facing such kind of situation. The uniform was very thin, and my body could be easily seen. They bought another sticker with the same code and pasted it on the locker in which my clothes were kept. They took me, and we went out. We started walking in a long corridor with a gate at the end. There was not much light. It was difficult to see the other person clearly. There were only guards with guns standing in alert position. We reached the gate. 2 guards were there with guns. They looked very scary. They had big black moustaches, which made me feel frightened. We reached the gate. One of my policemen asked the guard if he was not. 654, and jailer sir had allotted him bark no. 73. One of them took a register in his hand and started finding something. He asked, barking no. 73. One of my guards nodded his head. Then he said yeah, he has to stay with Chandan Singh and Lalit Sangar. Chandan Singh and Lalit Sangar were two new names for me, and I heard them for the first time. I asked my guard who these two people were. They replied that you have to stay with them starting today. The guards opened the gate, and we went in. There were barks from both sides, and there was a lot of noise. I saw inside the barks that only the criminals were fighting. When they saw me, they came on the iron grills of their barks and started teasing me. This made me very frightened. Every bark had its own number written on its top. I noticed a common thing there: without the guards, everyone was wearing the same uniform. We reached bark no. 72, and my heartbeat started getting high because I knew after it, there would definitely be bark no. 73. We again moved a little bit, and there was bark no. 73. When I saw it, it was a small room with four beds in it. I saw two people talking with each other on their beds. One of my guards told me these two men are Chandan Singh and Lalit Sangar, and you will stay in this bark with them. He told me to follow each and every rule of the jail. If I failed to obey the rules, I would get punished, and my sentence would be increased. We were waiting, and the two men inside the bark came near the grills and were keenly seeing. They were also new faces for me; likewise, I was also a new face for them. By looking at their faces, they were not looking at criminals. In the meantime, a guard came running towards us with a big bunch of keys in his hand. He started trying the keys on the door. After several attempts, ultimately, the door was opened. When the guard pushed the door, it made a strong voice, and the door was opened after a couple of weeks. We went in. The policemen made my hands free. One of them laughed in a bad manner at me, which made me irritated. The jail guard came and pointed at one of the beds and asked me from today; this bed is yours. Then I saw there was another door inside the room. The guard pointed to the door and then asked me if this was your washroom. The guard told me you will get breakfast at 8 am, lunch at 1 pm, and dinner at 8 pm. After this, he pointed towards a door between the main doors. To get your breakfast, lunch and dinner, you have to go to the dining hall from this door. It will be open three times a day. I was silent. I was not asking anything because I didn't know what I had to ask. They went out, closed the door, and put the lock on. I was seeing two new people, so I was frightened and could only see the bark. I went and sat on my bed. Chandan and Lalit also saw me, but they did not ask me anything. I didn't even know who Chandan was or who

Lalit was. I only knew their names and nothing else. After a while, both of them came to my bed. They introduced themselves to me. I also introduced myself to them. They were very frank to me. I asked them for what reason you are here. Chandan replied he told me his father was working at a shop, and one day, the shop owner slapped him without any reason, and he got frantic and killed him. Lalit said they were having a small piece of land, and the Zamindar annexed it. When I went to his field and asked him about it, his nephew came and started misbehaving with me, and a fight started, and he got injured. They asked me how I was there. The most common thing among us was that all of us were Dalits and were being depressed by the upper casts in one way or another. Just in 40 to 45 minutes, we became friends. After a while, a bell rang. I didn't know what it indicated. I thought there was a temple in the jail, and its bell had ranged. I told Lalit we could go for *pooja* here. He laughed and replied it was not a temple bell. He said this bell rings three times a day during breakfast, lunch, and dinner. This time, it has ranged for dinner, and after 2 or 3 minutes, the guard will come and open the door. The guard came and started opening all the barks one by one. Every prisoner was giving him *salam*. Before he came to our bark, Chandan asked me to give him *salam*. I asked him why I would give the guard *Salam*. He told me I will tell you later. The guard came, and we gave him salam, and he asked us to move quickly. I did not have the experience of going out of the door. It was too short to get out of it. One had to bend his body, and I didn't know it. I didn't bend my body, and my head got hurt by it. I went out, but my head started tingling because the door was made of iron. Anyway, I didn't pay any attention to it, and I ran towards Chandan and Lalit. They asked me if I was fine. I didn't give any answer. We were walking towards the dining hall. Chandan came close to me, put his hand on my shoulder, and asked me you have to give salam to the guard, and it is a rule here. He continued by saying that whenever you do not give the guard salam, he will not do anything with you, but indirectly, he will not leave any chance by which he can harm you. We reached near the dining hall. There was a big line of descendants entering the dining hall. We joined the line. The descendants at my back were pushing me as I was already having pain in my head, and the pushing increased it. Anyhow, we went in. It was a big hall full of descendants. I saw there were a lot of mosquitos. Lalit told me that every descendant has his own plate and spoon, which he has to get from the head chef. Lalit took me with him to the head chef. He was a strong man of 45, having no hair on his head. When he saw me, he reacted in a bad way, and then he took a plate and a spoon from a box and gave them to me. He asked from today, you will take this plate and spoon from here, and then you will again drop it here. I nodded my head, and we went again towards the dining hall, where Chandan was waiting for us. There was a big line of descendants waiting to take the food. There were two descendants who were giving food to the others. When we reached them, we saw a lot of mosquitos roaming around the food. I saw there were two big pots. One was filled with rice, and another was filled with vegetable curry. Only a few were in front of us, and then there was our number. Chandan was in the front, I was in the middle, and Lalit was in the back. There was a lot of noise because there were hundreds of descendants. Suddenly, a person entered, and everyone became silent. I didn't know who he was. He was not wearing the jail uniform. He was wearing a casual dress. He had two persons with him who were wearing the jail uniform. One of the persons who was giving the food took three boxes and gave them to that person's bodyguard. Lalit came close to my ear and told me that the person was known by the name of Munna bhai. He is a big gangster and has killed more than 100 people and has also kidnapped a minster once. He comes to the jail for some days to pass the time. Whenever he wants to go out, his lawyer comes, and he goes with him to date, and not a single guard has asked him to follow the rules. I was surprised. The waiter gave me some rice and some curry on my plate. We started finding a space where we could sit to eat dinner. Chandan found a table, and we went there. I saw that the chairs were all broken. Some had only two legs, and some were cracked in the centre. Anyhow, I took a chair and sat on it. Chandan and Lalit also sat down. I was thinking about the new name which I heard, Munna bhai. The rice was not cooked well. It still had pebbles in it. I started picking them up from the rice, and Chandan and Lalit also did the same. Chandan asked me this is our life. We have to accept it. Without accepting it, we have no other option. I didn't ask anything; I was sad about my family. When I was looking towards my dinner, I thought, how it is, it doesn't matter.

My family will not even have this for dinner due to me. At that time, I was having thousands of feelings in my mind which were emotionally hurting me. About 30% of the rice was pebbles. And in the remaining 70%, there were also pebbles, but I was hungry, so I didn't do anything with them. I mixed the curry with the rice. When I took the first bolus, it was watery, and there might have been no salt in it, and it didn't taste good. Anyhow, I ate it, but a little. I was not getting adjusted properly. I saw there was a bad environment; some were fighting, some were using rude language, and some were smoking. I noticed that some descendants were smoking in a corner of the hall, and no one was stopping them. I questioned Lalit about this. Lalit answered and told me they were the members of the Munna bhai gang, and that is why no one could stop them, and even the guards provided them with cigarettes to drink. I was very upset because I had never been in a situation like it was. I noticed that in jail, there was also discrimination among the descendants. Chandan told me that only 10 minutes were left for dinner time, so I had to finish my dinner quickly. I was not even able to swallow the food, but I was hungry also, so I ate it. Suddenly, I started getting hiccups. Lalit told me it was my first time eating the jail food, which is why it happened, and that it might last for 2 to 3 days or even more. I drank some water, and I got some relief. I was already irritated by the headache, and these hiccups increased my irritation. Chandan and Lalit took their plates as well as mine for washing and advised me to stay there till they came. I nodded my head, and they went to wash them. There was a big queue near the sink. I was only seeing Chandan and Lalit in the queue. Suddenly, a noise came, and when I saw back, there was a fight between two descendants. Everyone became silent, and everyone was only seeing them, but no one was stopping them. I was surprised. Both of them were injured, but still, they were fighting.

In the meantime, the guards came, but they were not able to control them. Anyhow, the fight stopped, and both of them were shifted to the hospital, but they were still trying to attack each other. The floor got red by the blood. In the meantime, Chandan and Lalit came. A bell rang. Chandan told me this bell was the indication for us that we had to go to our barks because dinner time was finished. We went towards the main door, and suddenly, a guard pointed his finger towards us and asked you 3, come here. We went to the guard. This time, he pointed his finger towards the floor, asked us to clean it and gave us the towels. I got frantic by it. I told him we were not there to clean the floors and it was not our work. His expression changed. He came near me and asked Chandan if he was new here and if he knew about the rules. Chandan started touching his feet and asked him to forgive me. I was going to talk again, and in the meanwhile, Lalit put his hand on my mouth and asked in my ear to be silent and clean it. The guard asked me you are new here, and your friend has begged me to forgive you. That is why I am forgiving you. The next time you are again questioned then, you will see what will happen to you. Then he asked me to clean the floor as soon as possible, and they moved towards your bark silently. After saying these words, he spat his paan on my uniform, smiled in a bad way and then went away. I was going to ask Chandan about this, and he asked me to remain silent and clean the floor. Lalit came close to me, and he also advised me to do the same that Chandan asked me to do and then told me we would talk about it in the bark. Chandan also nodded his head, and we started cleaning the floor with the towels. The towels had a very bad smell, and they were being used to clean the toilets. Anyhow, we finished the cleaning in 20 to 25 minutes. Chandan told Lalit and me that we should wash the towels first and then go to our bark. This time, I again got angry, but I remained silent. We washed the towels and put them on the shelf near the washroom. We went towards our bark. This time, when we were walking, there was silence all around. I got confused by it. Then I thought, might the descendants have slept? But when we reached the corridor, all the descendants were on the gates of the barks. Everyone was silent. There was only the sound of our walking and no other sound. We reached near our bark. Chandan and Lalit were also confused. The bark opposite ours had two descendants in it, Pankaj and Suresh. Lalit went silently towards that bark without coming under the surveillance of the guards. Suresh told something in Lalit's ear, and Lalit came back. We entered in our bark, and the guard locked it. We sat down. Lalit told us that today, Gullu Singh will be hanged to death. This silence is due to that. Lalit told me that Gullu Singh is a big gangster; he has committed 20 murders and also killed the police D.G.P. 1 month back. It was my first day in jail, and I was only coming across the names of different gangsters.

Chandan told me that if I had not asked the guard to forgive, he might have shifted to a dark cell. I told Chandan that if we were not here to clean the floors, then how could the guard force us to clean the floor? Lalit asked me this is jail, not your home. You have to only do what you are asked to do. You can't do what you like. I asked Chandan what the dark cell was. Chandan replied that a dark cell is like a bark in which you will be put alone, and there is no light. You will get the food only once time, and after every 3 hours, you will be tortured, whether by electric shocks or by 3rd-degree torture. Suddenly, a sound came off walking. Everyone became attentive. We sat on the door. Two guards were coming, and Gullu Singh was between them. Everyone was sad because everyone had seen Gullu Singh for the last time. But Gullu Singh looked comfortable, smiling at everyone. Gullu Singh was from Chandan's village, Seemapur. I didn't know it. Chandan went back to his bed and started weeping.

When Gullu Singh reached our bark, he asked the guards to stop and called Chandan. The guards were forcing him to move, but he ignored them. Chandan came close to the door, but tears were falling from his face. Gullu Singh told Chandan not to cry. It is called life, but promise me you will take care of my mother. I was not a criminal. My situation made me a criminal. I hope we will meet again. Chandan nodded his head, and Gullu went away, but he only saw back towards our bark. I told Chandan Gullu he was a murderer, a criminal. Then why are you weeping for him? Chandan said it is true that Gullu was a criminal, but he didn't become a criminal by his choice. Gullu was an efficient student of his time. His father worked in the police as a constable, but the police D.G.P didn't behave well with him due to his caste. Not only the D.G.P but the other officers also rebuked him. At last, he got totally frustrated, and he attempted suicide. After this incident, Gullu became a criminal. He killed all the officers, but after killing ten of them, he was arrested. After three months of his arrest, he fainted a guard and left the jail. He again went out. Then he killed the other officers also, and finally he killed the D.G.P and completed his revenge. After the killing, he surrendered on his own and accepted his crime, and then the court gave him the death sentence. After hearing the story of Gullu, a ray of hope was raised in me for taking revenge on the saith. The next morning, when we woke up, it was 6 am. We got fresh, and the breakfast bell rang. The guard opened us, and we went for breakfast. It was my second day in the jail. In the morning, I met many other descendants of different barks. For breakfast, we got a small cup of tea and a dry chapati. I saw a goon of Munna bhai come, and he brought breakfast for him. It was hurting me. We were eating these dry chapatis, and he was eating tasty dishes. Besides, he was also a descendant of ours. We went back to our bark. I was getting bored because it was my second day, and I was not still adjusting properly. Anyhow, the time passed till lunchtime. In the dining hall, Munna bhai came with his goons. Lalit was still in line waiting for the food. Munna went from there and pushed Lalit. Lalit asked nothing and got up. I got very much angry. I went to Munna and asked him to say sorry to Lalit. Everyone was surprised because everyone there was seeing anyone for the first time to question Munna. Munna smiled at me and took his hand to slap on my face. I blocked his hand and slapped him on his face. Everyone was shocked. His goons came to beat me, but he stopped them and told me, "I will see you," and went away without taking the lunch. I again came to my place and sat down, but everyone only saw me. I didn't give any attention to anyone. Chandan and Lalit were also scared. Chandan told me, "You are gone; he will not leave you." I told him I didn't care. I was right. How dare he push Lalit without any reason. We finished lunch but everyone present there only saw me.

Might I have achieved something big? I thought by slapping a gangster, these people were taking me seriously, really they were "mad.' We went towards our bark. All the descendants were giving me *salam*, not only me but also Chandan and Lalit. Lalit came close to my ear and told me, "This is your second day, and everybody is respecting you. You are really brave." I smiled at him but asked nothing. We went to our bark. We entered, but today, something was smelling different, and it was very strange that the guard had not locked the bark outside; besides, he was outside. I thought he might have forgotten it, and I didn't take it very seriously. Chandan told me, "I am smelling a rat here." I told him why. He answered to date. It was the first time when the guard had not locked us, and he was sitting outside. There was something that was going to happen. Becoming prey to confusion, it is better to ask the guard about it. Lalit went close to the door and saw a waiter, Subash, whispering with the guard. Lalit excused the guard and told him very politely that he had forgotten to lock us. In return, the guard asked nothing but smile at Subash. A call came to the guard, and he went away. Subash came to our bark and came silently inside. He asked Munna bhai to order the guard not to lock your bark because he wanted to take revenge for the slap from you and pointed his finger towards me. He went out. Lalit tried to stop him, but he went away. Lalit and Chandan panicked after hearing about the situation. Lalit started roaming in the bark. He asked if we save ourselves anyhow. If anything happens to us, then who will look after our families? They are already living in crucial situations, and this will give them a big shock. By hearing these words, I got emotional and started thinking about my family and what would happen to them after me. Chandan said, "Well" cool down. We will save ourselves. Lalit asked how we would save ourselves if they came here with their weapons and attacked us. Then what will we do? Chandan said if we are not here, then on whom they will attack. I got confused and came near to Chandan and asked if we could escape from there. He replied no. Lalit asked you are mad, Chandan. What do you want to say? Chandan asked nothing and looked to the roof. There was a fan that had about a centimetre of dust on it and was without power connections. Lalit asked Chandan what did you want to say actually. Chandan said we would hurt ourselves on our own, and then we would put the fan down if it injured us, and then we would be shifted to the hospital for some days. We agreed with Chandan and then started hurting ourselves till blood came out from different parts of our body, but it was hurting. Chandan said he would pull the fan down, and we had to scream together if it had fallen on its own. We did the same. Chandan pulled the fan down, and we started screaming. The fan was big, so it cracked the floor tiles, and we unscrambled it might have made us. First, two guards came and then four more guards. They called the Ambulance and started rescuing us. We were shifted to the hospital. The doctors gave us first aid and then shifted us to the ward. In the hospital, we were under the supervision of three cops. There were many other patients in the ward, but everyone was just seeing us because we were descendants. I was feeling very awkward to be unique among the patients. We were close to each other, but we were not able to talk to each other. The night passed away, and the sunlight made me wake up. Chandan and Lalit also woke up. The doctors came to inspect the patients. A doctor came to my bed and started inspecting me. A guard stood alert there. After inspecting me, he went to Chandan's bed and, after that, to Lalit's bed. Finally, he called a guard and said, "Well," they would be cured soon. Might they be discharged tomorrow or the day after tomorrow? After hearing these words, we got panic because the environment in the jail was not cool yet. We started seeing each other because we were frightened. The guards were going to be replaced by the other three guards because they had finished their shift. After a while, three new guards came, and the old ones went away. We were suspended. What to do now? Some ward boys came, and they started shifting the other patients to another ward. This situation made us panic. We thought we might be going to receive an attack from the Munna bhai gang. I was saying sorry to Chandan and Lalit because they were in such a situation because of me only. I was very scared. There were thousands of bad thoughts roaming in my mind. Finally, I dared to ask a guard about this situation. He didn't reply even though he didn't give any attention to me. Suddenly, some men entered, and the guards were alerted. They came to me and told me Rana bhai wanted to meet you. I didn't know who he was because I heard the name for the first time in my life. I asked Lalit about this. When Lalit heard the name, he was completely shocked. He said that Rana bhai is a high-level gangster. He has committed thousands of crimes and has a strong rivalry with Munna bhai. I wondered why he wanted to meet a person like me who didn't even know anything about the criminal world. The guards, as well as the goons, got alert because Rana bhai was going to enter. My nervousness was at a high-level. My body was strong, shivering. I was confused and stressed; I didn't even know how to react. Suddenly a tall man came wearing a black dress and had long hair in different colours. One of his goons pointed his finger towards me. Rana bhai came to me and sat down on a chair. He put his hand on my shoulder and started smiling. He continued and said that he knew everything about me. I was silent because it was the first time in front of such a big criminal. He told me that he was totally impressed by me. I got confused about how he was impressed by me. He told me, "I am impressed by you. You are a brave person. Without caring about anything, you slapped the bloody Munna." When I heard these words, I felt some relief. He continued and said you are not a murderer. You are under a fake case here. I was surprised after hearing these words. He said the person with whom you had the fight had not died. He is alive. He was just injured and nothing else. I told him then why I was there. He said the *saith* with whom you were having a rivalry had made a fake case against you to depress you and your family. After hearing these words, I was shocked. My blood was getting heated. He offered me to join his gang. I did not have any other option than to join him. He told me that I would be free from jail with Chandan and Lalit, and if they wanted, they could also join my gang. They also agreed to join the gang. He told me that we would be discharged from the hospital and in jail, and his goons would protect us. I was happy and thanked him a lot, and he went away with a smile on his face. Chandan and Lalit were also happy. Now, my only motive was to take revenge on the saith. After a couple of hours, we were discharged from the hospital. We were again shifted to the jail. When we reached the jail, the news was already spread that we had joined with Rana bhai. When we reached the corridor, everyone only saw us with open eyes because, for the criminal world, it was really a big achievement. We were now put in another bark where the goons of Rana bhai were locked. They started welcoming us. When we went for lunch, all the descendants came out of the queues and gave us space, and among the descendants, some were also from the upper castes. It was the first time in my life that anyone respected me. Some days passed, and a new lawyer came with bail for us. Now it was the time when I was going to leave the jail. Chandan and Lalit were thanking me because they were going out of jail. They were meeting their other friends because they had spent a lot of time in the jail. We were told to take the uniform out, and we were given new clothes to wear, which were sent by Rana bhai through our lawyer. I took my old clothes with me because they were bought by my mother so there was no chance of leaving them there, so I took them with me. When we reached out of the jail, a big car was waiting for us. It was the first time I sat in a car in my life. We reached a big villa beyond my expectations. We went in. It was very beautiful inside. We sat down. Lunch was offered to us, and there were several varieties. We had lunch happily. We were now asked to do some rest till Rana bhai came back home. We waited for some time, and Rana bhai came. He sat down with us. He told me now you have entered the criminal world. You are now not a common man. He told us that from tomorrow, we have to go and collect the extortion from the upper caste rich people. The next day, we went and collected the extortion, and it had become an art for me. I did it for a couple of months, and I started to deal with weapons and day by day, I was becoming a professional criminal. Now, there was a strong name for me in the area. Now, my family was also happy because they were living luxurious lives. I now only had one motive to take my revenge from the saith. One day, I took seven cars and 17 goons with me to the saiths house. We were all having weapons with us. When we reached first, we killed all the goons of the saith, and then we went inside. First, I killed his whole family and then went inside his room. When he saw me, he got nervous and started crying. I opened fire, and six bullets were pierced in his heart. He was dead now. I ordered one of my goons to spit paan on his face. We went out and burnt his whole house. I went in my car towards our house. Now, I have taken my revenge, which was my motive, but I was only thinking one thing: "What made me a criminal?"